*The Holy Man
and Other Stories*

The Holy Man
and Other Stories

Alexander Trocchi

CALDER

CALDER PUBLICATIONS
an imprint of

ALMA BOOKS LTD
3 Castle Yard
Richmond
Surrey TW10 6TF
United Kingdom
www.calderpublications.com

These stories first published together with *Young Adam* in *Outsiders* by
New American Library of World Literature in 1961. Republished as
'Four Stories' in *New Writers 3* by John Calder (Publishers) Ltd in 1965
This edition first published by Calder Publications in 2019

Cover design by Will Dady

Printed in Great Britain by CPI Group (UK) Ltd, Croydon CR0 4YY

ISBN: 978-0-7145-4847-0

Contents

The Holy Man
and Other Stories

A Being of Distances

I T WAS BEHIND NOW – the station, the yellow steam. The train moved slowly out of the terminus, sidled against signalboxes, abandoned trucks, and then, incongruously, where a wall fell away, against palely lit windows in a tenement. Glimpses of rusted gutters, of garish wallpaper – but there was life there, or it was curtained off and not to be seen: hoardings, *Gordon's Gin*, *Aspro*, *Sandeman's Fine Old...* until he felt the train pulled away again by the rails into a new direction.

It was nearly dark, and the old man whose face had aged in the last half-hour and with whom he had walked along the platform was in the past, beyond him.

Soon then the spokes of the city rotated and fell away from the carriage window, and gradually an uneasiness in his own body, the rhythm of the wheels on the rails came to him – his mind on his father without image – and then from somewhere ahead, like a hound straining at a leash, the thin scream of the engine as it thrust more quickly into open country.

He stretched his legs and noticed the mud in the crevices of his shoes. The girl sitting opposite was wearing a red coat. He noticed that first, and then the dull turnip-like sheen of her heavy legs and the self-conscious feet in shoes of worn black suede. Tired feet, arched whitely, awkward. A spent match lay beside her left foot. He did not look up – he was conscious that he was pretending to look at the carriage floor – and soon the legs became merely a lustre on which he was aware of the fine sensitive antennal quality of hairs. He was sorry then that he had stepped onto the train.

For his father would be alone now. And soon he would turn on the light in his room and be alone. But in the end – her legs were crossed at the knees, her black skirt where the coat fell apart was drawn tightly above the kneecap against the flesh – in the end, it would always be like that: no intrusion of his own would alter it. To get to a man it was necessary to accept his premises, and with his father that had been impossible. He had been unable to say "It won't be long", because he was sick of his own voice, of dissimulation, and anyway both he and his father had known – "Next time it will be for me" – when they glanced at each other that afternoon at the grave of the uncle.

The coffin had brass fittings and smelt of varnish. It had been supported by scrubbed deal-wood trestles in the middle of the room, the "blue" room, and had dominated the room as an altar dominates a small church, blue pillars, and over it all was the smell of flowers and death and varnish – like the smell of cider apples, he had thought – which set the mourners at a distance from the dead man far more utterly than his mere dying had. The smell pervaded the whole house, met one at the door, and as the mourners arrived in their white collars and black ties, shaking their hands, talking in hushed tones, nodding to others distantly known, it had descended on them, crystallizing their emotion, and drawn them inexorably towards the room given over to death.

In the room he had glanced from the waxlike face of the dead man upwards at the tall blue curtains with their faded silver flowers, trying to recognize again the familiarity of ten years before, when, down from the university, he had sat there on one of the blue chairs and told his uncle that he would no longer be interested in accepting an appointment with the firm. The uncle, a man nearing sixty at the time, showed no surprise – like father, like son, Philip's child – said shortly he was disappointed: "...thought you'd turn out more like *our* side of the family" – and when Christopher did not reply: "but you seem to have made up your mind..."

"Yes," Christopher said, "it's quite definite."

"I'm sorry about that," his uncle said, "and in spite of our differences I think your father will be disappointed too." He had felt like saying then that it was not for his father that he was doing it, not even for the *other* side of the family, but at that moment for his father, who had felt bitter against the uncle and against Jack and Harry... Harry who brought to everything his soul of a piano accordion.

Now, in the room beside the dead man, and his gaze falling from the long blue curtains, he had felt no bitterness, only perhaps a vague sense of disgust and a strong desire to be outside in the open street and away from the cloying sacramental odour of flowers and death in the suburban room.

Neither he nor his father had been invited to be pall-bearers. They had watched from a distance as the coffin was lowered into the grave, tilting, from silk cords, and then, following the example of others, they had each thrown a handful of dirt and cut grass on the lid of the coffin – a flat hollow sound from distended fingers, rain on canvas; did the dead man hear? Afterwards, the group of mourners stood back and the clergyman led a prayer: a small man with a bald head who had donned his trappings at the graveside – and when, without music, he had broken nervously with his small voice into the 121st Psalm and the mourners had taken it up, their voices ineffectually suspended like a wind-thinned pennant between earth and sky. Christopher glanced directly at his father, and for a second they had understood one another.

His father dropped his gaze first, almost involuntarily, and Christopher looked beyond the mourners across the green slope, where the grey and white gravestones jutted upwards like broken teeth.

After the prayers and the singing, the two work-men moved forwards self-consciously and threw the earth back into the grave, and the long block of raised earth was covered with wreaths. The clergyman shook hands with the family, muttered an apology and went with his little leather case alone down the path without looking back.

Harry was there, puffy and self-important as usual, and Jack as though now that their father was buried they had noticed him for the first time, and there was talking and questions: how was he? Were things going well? Lucky devil to live abroad these days! Over-hearty, evasive. Was it not funny how everything had turned out differently, not as one expected? And he supposed they were refer-ring to his clothes, informal and beginning to be threadbare – poor old Chris, gone the way of his father – his general air of anonymity.

"Come and see us before you go," Jack had said vaguely, but he was already signalling to his wife that he would join her in a moment. "Don't forget now, old man, Catherine would *love* to hear all about your travels, always talking about you. See you soon then – before you go, Marco Polo, eh? – sure, and give my regards to your father, do."

"You should have told him to keep them" – and Christopher looked round, and his father was standing at his elbow – small, grey, inconspicuous – and he said again: "You should have told him to keep them, Christopher. Why should I accept his regards through you?"

"Forget it, Dad. They're not worth thinking about."

"The last time any of them spoke to me was fifteen years ago, nine years after your mother died. It was on Armistice Day. I remember, because I bought a poppy…"

"Don't worry about it."

"There's a reception," his father said. "We were not invited."

"Would you have wanted to go anyway?"

"Not really, no."

"Well, then."

"Next time," his father said when they were alone, "it will be for me."

"I'll be back soon. I promise."

He had thought then that it was hardly a lie; there was no way of knowing.

They lingered after the other mourners were gone, walking along the gravel footpaths between the graves, and the grave of the uncle with its covering of bright wreaths was nearly out of sight.

"Your mother was buried here," his father said. "Would you like to see the grave?"

"Not particularly," he said after a moment's hesitation.

"You've never visited it."

"No. I never have. Would you like a drink?"

"It's just as you wish," his father said without looking at him, "but I thought as we were here anyway..."

"No, Dad. I don't want to."

Springtime, he was thinking. To be in England. Casually he stooped to pick up a broken flower which had fallen on the path. It was quite fresh.

"From a wreath," his father said.

"Probably."

They walked slowly, in silence, and the sky was low and white-grey, like milk which has stood for a long time in a cat's saucer collecting dust, and as he looked up he felt a raindrop on his face. "Looks as though it's going to rain," he said.

"I come here every month," his father was saying. "Sometimes I miss a month, but not often. It's the least I can do."

In Christopher the impulse to say something died. He glanced at him, but his father avoided his eye, and there was a faint flush on his cheeks. It was as though his father had said: "I'm old now, Chris, you must understand" – said that and not the other thing, which was not important and which was not really what he had wanted to say. And Christopher wanted to put his arm round him and to say "We're like one another, Dad" – does he expect me to? – but he could not make the gesture.

His father was looking at him uncertainly.

"I've sometimes wondered, Chris, why you didn't go into the business – your uncle's, I mean."

"Have you?"

"You'd have been independent today. Take Jack and Harry."

"I *am* independent."

A gust of wind then – how naked the cemetery was!

"Of course. I know," his father said. "But you know what I mean."

"Money?"

Coughing, "And position, you know. Your cousins are both in good positions now."

"Do you envy them?"

"Who? Me?"

His father's laugh sounded false and forced. Christopher looked away at an urn on a pillar of white marble; the inscription was in Latin... *in vitam æternam,** he read.

"You know that's not true, son."

"Why bring it up then?" He added more quietly: "I don't like them, and I don't like talking about them."

"It's just as you wish," his father said. "I didn't mean to upset you, Chris, you know that. It's just that sometimes... well, I think it was your birthright. Your mother was his sister, after all."

"And you're my father."

He had meant it to be a statement of fact only, but his father had crumpled and his mouth had fallen open. Then he had had an impulse to explain himself to his father – he would not have had it otherwise, at no point would he gladly have gone back on the past, didn't he see? – but he would not have understood. "We're alike, son, you and I." He might have said that. His son, after all. The second generation.

"I realize, of course," his father said at last, "that I've stood in your way. You shouldn't have let me, Chris."

He would always believe that – my son, my world – holding on to them like men held on to their dead, with words and memories of words. *Perducat nos in vitam æternam.**

He found himself saying: "You needn't blame yourself, Dad. You didn't really stand in my way" – and he was going to add: "It wasn't you who decided me, not at all", but the smile of disbelief was already there, like a visor over the eyes.

They walked on.

And now he noticed that his father's hat looked too big for him. It did not fit him. And he took his father's arm.

"Your hat's too big for you, Dad!"

The old man laughed. "Can't afford another, Chris! D'you know, when I bought my first hat, they cost twelve and six – the best, mind you. The same hat costs sixty-two and six today. The cheap ones are no good, no good at all... *This* is a Borsalino."

A Borsalino. His father had halted, removed his hat and pointed with his forefinger at the discoloured silk lining (pomade, a little jar of green stuff in the bathroom cabinet). "Borsalino. Made in Italy. You see?"

"Must be a good one."

"The best," his father said.

They were walking towards the main gate of the cemetery.

The cortège had already broken up, and the last of the cars was gone. The gate porter nodded to them as they walked out onto the street.

"I suppose those shops do good business?" Christopher said to his father, referring to the row of shops which sold graveside ornaments and flowers. "Like bookstalls in railway stations." A point of departure.

"Capital," his father said. "I bought a vase there once for your mother's grave, but one day when I went back somebody had broken it. That's over two years ago now... yes, must be that at least."

"And shells," Christopher said.

"Yes. You can buy shells with inscriptions."

"Pink ones," Christopher said, and he smiled, but his father was looking straight ahead and walking quickly, as he always did on the street, and he seemed to have forgotten what they were talking about.

"Will you go abroad again immediately?"

"I suppose so," Christopher said. "There's nothing for me here – you know that, Dad."

"I know."

"I may spend a day or two in London."

"And then where? France?"

"North Africa, perhaps."

"Was there during the first war," his father said. "Alex."

"Yes."

"I know! It was the day before your aunt Eleanor died."

"What was?"

"The day I found the vase broken. Sheer vandalism."

"Yes, it was a pity."

"I paid seventeen and six for it. It wasn't cheap. Come on, we'll get a drink across the road there." And they crossed the street towards the green-painted public house.

It had been easy there, with a glass of whisky in front of them, to recreate the surface intimacy which, ten years before, he had assented to during a game of billiards – "never pot your opponent's ball" – their having even then little to talk about, and their inexpertness at the game causing them to smile, to laugh, to be together, until, in the sun again, they had taken leave of one another before they grew apart, Christopher to go to a class at the university, his father to drink coffee in some smoke room or other and to read and reread the local paper.

His father had talked and lived again memories of Cairo, Jaffa – the oranges were tremendous, like small melons – and Suez, spoken of a head wound he had received, shrapnel – fingering his scalp tenderly – and which had resulted in his being "sent down the line" to the base hospital and thence home to "Blighty", and as his father uttered the word lovingly, Christopher wondered how he could have failed to relate that homecoming to those things to which he *came* home... or did he come home? For it seemed to Christopher that those years and those vague memories were the only positive thing in his father's life – he invariably returned to them after a few drinks – and that from the day he had set foot again in England he had known nothing but humiliation. The successful brother-in-law, the dead wife, the son (Christopher) who was brought up in a world in which one could refer to his father only in a discreet whisper and never in the presence of guests, his father's debts, his pride, his humiliation before the brother of his dead wife and his gradual and, in practice, final exclusion from the world into which he had married: those were the things to which his father returned and to which, sitting there in the bar, he could refer incongruously as "Blighty".

"Those were the days, Chris! You were too young, of course. Good Scotch, what was it? Seven and six a bottle, yes..." Jaffa oranges, pick them off the trees, get a native to do it for your ackers, the price of second-hand furniture, "...too bad you're not setting up house, know where you could get some cheap" – a dealer, Silverstein, good business in the East End, trust the Jews – "...see a man was convicted at the Old Bailey, *fif*teen thousand gold watches – that's smuggling!" – no wonder income tax, bloody robbers – conversation which always in the end returned to the same theme, the *deaths* column in the local paper, as though the printed notices informed him, quietly bringing desolation to his eyes, that time was running out.

"Did you know old Macarthy, Chris? The one who left three hundred thousand? The widow, Hargreave's girl, 's gone to the Riviera – didn't do so bad for herself. Can't be more than thirty-nine."

His father didn't talk much during dinner – "the doctor says to cut down on eats" – dabbing with the napkin at his shrunken potato-like mouth and chin – and later, at the railway station, he did not look round. He was still carrying the local paper with its columns of births and deaths, carrying the living and the dead, and he walked quickly across the main hall of the station past the bookstall. His head momentarily in profile, his hat *was* too big for him, and then his back walking away. His son watched him go and returned along the platform to the waiting train. The guard had already whistled, and as Christopher boarded the train he became aware that some soldiers were singing in the next compartment. Song, not words, the umbilical chord. Poor old man...

The train lurched over points and steadied against the flickering ribbon of another train which flared past in the opposite direction. Their noises merged and separated. And then the countryside was dark.

After everything, the unexpected arrival, the funeral, the departure just as unexpected – because he felt "impelled" to go – he was the same man. The noise of the wheels on the rails moved in on him and treacherously his thoughts crystallized. He had not the faintest idea why or where he was going.

Going to the past, remembering places he had gone to and come away from, and the passage of time, he felt very cut off, and more unsure of himself, now he was approaching middle age, than he had ever been before. He had stepped aboard because the momentary impulse to run after the retreating figure of his father had seemed silly. Tomorrow or the next day he would have been at the station again.

The smoke from the girl's cigarette made him look at her face. She was not much more than twenty, fair, with a rather heavy face and unexpressive grey eyes. She was looking out of the window and pretending to be unaware of him. There was no one else in the carriage. Ten years ago he would have tried to seduce her.

That made him think that she reminded him of something – a gramophone in a hotel bedroom in Oslo and a woman with heavy limbs, a melody which cried out in a little boxy voice; and the red neon sign at the opposite side of the street was visible, confederate, at the small window.

From a brown paper bag on her knee the girl had taken an orange and was peeling it. She dropped the bits on the floor and pushed them with her heel out of sight under the seat, carefully. He noticed now that she had thick ankles and that the straps of her shoes bit into the flesh, which bulged over them like fungus over the edge of wood. She opened up a newspaper between herself and him before she ate the orange.

And his uncle too had been pink and somehow angry when he was living (an undertaker's colour in his coffin), and he had said in his serious, unsurprised voice, "I'm sorry about that," and looked for the only reason he understood to explain the attitude of the young man who faced him in the "blue" room without explanation. And so for the world of his uncle he was his father's son, a chip off the old block, and everything was simple and understandable and in no way implied criticism of that world.

The girl opposite was still pretending to be unaware of him, and yet she was aware – and there it was, as effective as words, a decision, an act, which he had rejected before and which he would continue to reject wherever it met up with him, which had driven him out of the world of the cousins and the uncle into his own isolation.

In the morning he would be in London. Nothing isolated him more than Victoria Station, especially in the morning, when the local trains came and thousands of office workers moved across the hall to the various exits. He had stood not more than a week before drinking tea in the rail bar and watched until the stragglers had left the station. Afterwards, he had decided over again.

He could not remember making the decision. It had been there all the time. He found himself not part of, and therefore driven to reject, the world into which he had been born. His father could say: "Most of the old gang are gone now" because he had need of the words, now he was growing old, and because he was part of a generation in society which was dying, a few each month in the *deaths* column of the local paper. But if his father were alone, it was not because his contemporaries were dead.

Neither of us had contemporaries.

Like father, like son – even unto the third and fourth, the dead man knew.

Christopher rested his head against the back of the seat and lit a cigarette. His own wound, knife, his own decision. He rejected the women who would have married him and borne his children, he rejected the men who would have employed him and those who would have been employed under him. He rejected war and peace, and the artificial truss of all opposites which men died for or fought against. There could never be a retraction, because whatever he looked at was false. "Most of the old gang" were not dead for him, because they had never existed. Sometimes he watched men or women or traffic in the streets, but always from the outside, and with the same feelings with which he would have listened to a story which had no point; and yet there they were – everything, everyone, each under his umbrella, each under his own lie of significance.

A man came in out of the corridor through the sliding door. Christopher glanced away from him and rubbed the window with his sleeve. The train had halted at a station. When he looked back into the carriage, the man nodded to him, smiled to the girl and put a briefcase on the rack. He had a red face which had the appearance of being too much soaped in hot water. He sat down near the girl.

Christopher turned back to the window. He thought that now his father would have turned on the electric fire and would be pouring over the *deaths* column like a speculator over a stock-market bulletin. Later he would make tea for himself and drink it, looking at the two bars of the electric fire – "Damn chilly just now" – and then he would get up, wash the cup and saucer and prepare in detail, reluctantly, to go to bed. If I hadn't gotten onto the train, Christopher thought, I could have stayed a few more days with him.

"—for holidays," the girl was saying.

"Not very good weather," the man said.

"You're telling me!" She glanced at Christopher and, as though he had caught her at something, flushed.

He looked out of the window, but it was too dark to see anything – sometimes, only, a patch of cinders from the engine, lambent, isolated.

Later, all three occupants dozed.

The train ran over rails with a monotonous voice into minutes and hours between night in two towns. In the compartment, the windows were misted and the air was cold with the coldness of the unsheathed electric-light bulb. On one seat the girl dozed uneasily with her head on the shoulder of the red-faced man. On the other seat, the man who had left his father for no reason was carried with his absurd thought of a window perspiring on the Riviera into distances from which he would always – until one day, perhaps with words, and because he feared death – be excluded.

The Holy Man

THE HOTEL WAS LOCATED in a short impasse near the Bal des Anglais. The street face bulged outwards and upwards from street level, receding again after the first storey like a long narrow forehead, until it was cut short by the sky-line. Back from the ridge of the roof, out of view from the street, there was a single attic window, and above it an uneven row of dilapidated chimney pots, yellow and black, and tilted in oblique postures. There was no break in the tenement structure of the street, and the hotel was distinguishable from the buildings on either side only by its more pronounced bulge and by the peeling yellow paint which covered its outside wall.

It was not a light street. The sun seldom perco-lated downwards beyond the second storeys and, except for a month or so during the summer, the street at ground level was in shadow. There was life in the street, and an occasional outraged cat, but more than anything else it was a street to die in.

The ground floor of the hotel had at one time been a bar, frequented by North Africans and by the prostitutes of the quarter, and it remained shopfronted. Above, the windows, tilting at various angles from the perpendicular, looked out, through absence of sun and through grime, like the mucous eyes of some of the blind or half-blind men who in latter days came to stay there. Access to the passage which led to the staircase was by a single narrow door. A man entering from the sunless street into a darker corridor, which smelt of dampness and urine and decaying ordure, was in a passage twenty feet long; on his left immediately was the yellow slit of light which came from under the door – the

former back door – of what used to be the bar.
Through that door, often, and especially at night,
came female laughter. The room was inhabited
by three German women who had come to France
with the victorious army and who, like other odds,
ends and chevrons of the defeated army, had been
ambiguously left there. Their names were Liza,
Greta and Lili.

The staircase at the end of the corridor was a
wooden one. Its steps, worn smooth and concave
by centuries of climbing feet, had absorbed grease,
dust, sputum and spilt water until their surface
was like soft graphite. What fell soaked in and
remained. Halfway between landings, at the turn
of flights, the water spouts dripped into iron bowls
inadequately gridded against garbage, which sank
to the drains and caused each bowl to overflow its
contents onto the stairs below. The rooms were
small. Except for those which gave onto the street,
their windows opened onto an airwell which was

their only source of light. One of the rooms on the second storey was inhabited by a thin Hungarian. All night he stood near his uncurtained window, old and stark naked, and a candle flame ranged across the skin and hairs of his little abdomen as he picked over and examined the rags he had collected the previous day. His room was full of old clothes, but, except when going abroad into the streets, he did not use them. Sometimes he spat through a broken pane, and his spittle descended down the airshaft to its bottom below street level, where broken boxes, discarded bed springs and other debris were piled. When he did so, he leant forwards slightly, with an air of attention, as he listened for the sound of its break...

Opposite him on the second storey, with a window that gave directly onto his, lived a one-legged woman nearly as old as himself, a native of the city. Her muffled curses rose to the other inhabitants up the airwell. Sometimes the Hungarian paused in his task of inspection and gazed with his one good eye – the other had receded into what was now a pink rim of hair – across to the lightless window where she cursed. Each morning, before seven, she hobbled downstairs with her crutch close at her left armpit and the thong of her amputated leg in a grey woollen stole just visible below the hem of her skirt. Her face was twisted in a fixed red sneer, and her free hand against the wall prised her torso into balance as it descended. In the roadway she looked this way and that before she set off, like a bent hinge, always in the same direction.

Apart from the German women – and they were all over thirty – no young people lived there, and as the old died off or moved to the almshouse or to the sanatorium, or to prison for petty theft or chronic alcoholism, no young people presented themselves to occupy the rooms. Always another old man or another old woman, younger or older than the previous tenant, but old, and often emaciated. Already there lived in the rabbit warren of five storeys one hunchback, one dwarf too old for the circus, one strong man too weak to break chains, two blind men whose white probes brushed walls and stairs to the side or in front of them like antennae of insects, one dumb man and the woman already mentioned with the amputated foot. For the rest, they came and they went, on foot and sometimes on a stretcher. And not long ago a man died on the stairs.

But above all, and of a power that was intact because it was undivined, there was the holy man.

Why this man was holy, or what holy was, none of the other tenants was quite clear. That they were one and all willing to concede his holiness was quite clear from the fact that all referred to him – and without a trace of humour – as "the holy man".

He was above all the others, not only in the sense that he suffered from no physical disability – at least, if he did, no one knew about it – nor because he neither had nor appeared to require means of subsistence, nor even because he was admittedly holy, but also in the sense that he was above them in space, for it was he who inhabited the tiny attic room at the apex of the house, a room which, were it not for the fact that he had shuttered the dormer window with boards painted black, alone of the rooms in the hotel commanded an uninterrupted view of the sun and of the blue heavens.

The holy man had shut out the sun and the blue heavens from his room. He came years before, almost beyond living memory, clad in a dark mantle against recognition. Accepting the key from Mme Kronis, proprietress, he had mounted the stairs for the first and for the last time. He had carried with him a black blind of wood of the exact dimensions of the attic window, and with a hammer and nails he had boarded himself into darkness like a vegetable. From that day onward he had never set foot on stairs, nor for all they knew on ground or floor, but had lain in a prone position beneath a grey blanket on a narrow bed like a long cocoon.

It was known – or, if not known, suspected – that he had occupied this horizontal position for more than ten years in his black box at the apex of the hotel.

Now, none of the tenants loved the sun, unless it was the German women who, during the short period of the year when the sun struck down to street level, sprawled untidily on their doorstep (that of what had once been the bar) and scratched the pendulous deathly white flesh of their thighs which, in their reclining position with knees up, called out, like jaws, at the sun. But evidently no one hated the sun as much as the holy man, not the thin Hungarian nor any of the tenants who went abroad daily to beg in those parts of the city frequented by tourists during the summer. For a beggar in summer must sweat, and those who laid down their truncated limbs near the bridges where the tourists congregated did so in full sunlight, that the sweat might aggravate the emaciation, and the horror the charity.

And so at the beginning this strange hibernation, in spite of its occurrence in the twilit catacomb where all flesh was white from lack of sun, caused a great deal of comment, and various theories were advanced throughout the years to make it less foreign to the general comprehension.

The first was the obvious one: the man was dead.

Such an explanation would have occasioned less dismay than any other. To live, to grow old and to die: the process excited little interest. Those acquaintances who were not already dead were dying, or were preparing to die in the near future or in the winter, for most of them felt that they could hold out at least until the winter and the frost. It was true that few died in the hotel. The man who died on the stairs, a vast man from Lille with a mountain of weight to carry up five flights of stairs, had been taken by a spasm during his climb. That had been unexpected, the sudden thump around midnight as his body toppled backwards down the narrow staircase, but he had been drinking heavily and he had a bad heart – usually he had climbed very slowly, taking a few steps at a time. For the most part they went away to die, to the almshouse or to the sanatorium, and if somebody came round to enquire about a vacant room, Mme Kronis would say she was expecting a key in a few days' time. For each dead man, a key; it was usually returned to her by a policeman who climbed up the stairs behind her to make an inventory of the effects of the deceased. Later she would say if questioned: "His key came back today. There's a key, if you want it."

But it was not unnatural for a man who was about to die to make a crypt of his room. The sun was an irrelevance. If the holy man had died, it was as well he had died in darkness. A man wanted to die with a little dignity. Dark made that easier. It shut out the world.

Yes, it would have been easy to believe that the holy man was dead, had it not been for the stubborn recurrence of the symptoms of life. A hundred little facts combined to make the theory untenable.

In the first place, and perhaps most significantly of all, there was no key. Secondly, there was the direct evidence of the German women. For a number of years past, Liza, Greta and Lili, in strict rotation and in complete submission to some unknown authority, had borne his food and later removed his excrement. It was true, or so they said, that they had never seen the holy man. The room was in total darkness. Sometimes they had tried to make conversation, but the mass on the bed – their only experience of that mass was the sound of heavy breathing – remained inert and voiceless; nevertheless, they were aware of him. There was something there, they said: you could feel it on your skin, and the fetor of the place was suffocating. All the air that got in must have been with their exits and entrances, so the stench aroused neither disgust nor disbelief in the other tenants. It was interesting, but not important.

Of course, the German women might have been lying. But that they should lie over a number of years, climbing daily to the attic with food for a dead man (or a non-existent man) to relieve themselves up there in order to be able to return with the chamber pot, seemed unlikely. It was laughable – unless they had murdered him and were trying to cover up for themselves. That theory was suggested and caused so much indignation among the tenants that a few of them got together and, without consulting Mme Kronis, brought a policeman to the hotel. In spite of her protests, the policeman insisted on going to the room to see for himself. She allowed him to do so only on the condition that the rest of the tenants would remain below, and they heard her bicker about interference and lying thieves as she climbed slowly and painfully upwards ahead of the policeman.

It did not take long. A few moments later, the policeman descended and without a word went off into the night. A short while afterwards, Mme Kronis herself came down, still muttering under her breath, and disappeared into her room, locking the door behind her.

The procession of days continued uninterrupted – during which, as usual, Liza, Greta and Lili bore food and carried refuse to and from the holy man. Some said Mme Kronis had bribed the policeman. That was quite possible. Mme Kronis was rich and policemen were human. Was it not so? But, generally speaking, the tenants were convinced. The holy man was alive, even if his life were not what one would expect of a man – it was more like the life of a slug or of a bedbug – what did it matter? Perhaps he had gone up there to die and had not died after all, or was dying but was taking a long time over it. That would have been commendable. They were all of the opinion that a man should take a long time over his dying.

And perhaps that was what it was: he was merely taking a long time over his dying. He had boxed himself into his death chamber in anticipation of his immediate death, and then, finding each time he woke up that he still lived, he had concluded he would die on the morrow, and therefore had not troubled to take down the shutter that shut him off from the sun and from the blue sky. That would have been proper. After having outlived for so long his expectations, it would have been a shame to be caught napping with the shutter down. He might even have had a stroke if he had made the great effort that would have been required to tear down a shutter so firmly fixed with long nails. He was presumably no jackass or half-wit who wanted to die before it was strictly necessary to do so.

On the other hand – it was the thin Hungarian who suggested this – it was quite possible that the holy man thought he was dead. That would have accounted too for his passivity. If he thought he were dead, he would also think, and logically, that there was no need to act, neither to act nor to decide to act, for he would most certainly be of the opinion that the will – the personal will as distinct from the all-embracing will of God – ceased to be effective after death. And the fact that he had existed in darkness over a period of so many years would naturally conduce to the belief that he was suspended in Purgatory to await God's final judgement. That, the thin Hungarian thought, would explain everything, including the deaf ear he turned to the husky-voiced conversation of the German women – which, as he was now dead and beyond the failings of the flesh, he would most certainly interpret as the hallucinatory temptation of that part of his soul on whose account he was condemned to Limbo. He would be afraid to be taken in by his hallucinations, because if he were so taken in it would prove his basic carnality beyond a doubt – and that proven beyond the grave even, he would feel himself in imminent danger of being toppled right out of Limbo into something much worse. The holy man, the Hungarian concluded, was wise as well as holy.

The theory of the woman who had her foot amputated was less subtle, and, on those rare occasions when she ventured beyond her monotonous blasphemies to express an opinion, hers was expressed with hard and brittle conviction. The holy man was no more or less than the Devil himself, right on top of us, God knew; the German women, all three of them, were witches as well as Germans, and should have been burned.

The German women, indeed, were not popu-
lar – never had been since ambiguously they had
come to be there. In relation to the holy man, they
were suspected of withholding information. That
itself was exasperating, and grounds enough for
dislike. But that was not all. Their full bodies and
their thick loud laughter was out of place. It was
the laughter of the living against the condemned;
it seemed highly unlikely that they would be dying
soon, and probable that they would outlive the
rest by half a century. A female tenant could not
be expected to forgive that insult. A male tenant
might and, when alone, did more often than not,
for was he not a man before he was old?

The summers passed and, after the autumns,
the winters and the springs. No one again sent
for the police on the holy man's behalf. Indeed, in
the course of the years he was seldom referred to.
During the winters more keys became available. The
percentage was always higher during the winters.

Among others were the keys of the hunchback, of the dwarf too old for the circus, of the strongman too weak to break chains and of one of the blind men who, crossing a boulevard, got accidentally run over by a bus. Tenants came, tenants went, some to die, others to linger on. During the summers, Liza, Greta and Lili lounged on their doorstep, their fat thighs exposed and their broad haunches warm from the warm stone under them. They joked with the North Africans, winked or guffawed at a stray tourist and amused themselves by scratching and comparing their knees. At one point each day, one of them did the chores for the holy man, Liza or Greta or Lili, climbing up stairs which, in former days and with a strange man's eyes following the slow swing of her haunches, she had climbed for other purposes. All the year round, discreetly, they received visitors in their room, which used to be the bar, or alternatively went with them to the hotel round the corner, for some men, sometimes, prefer privacy in lovemaking. The thin Hungarian continued to exhibit his nakedness to those who faced him across the airwell, to pick at his rags, to spit and wait as a bird might and to elaborate his theory of the holy man. Daily he pushed a small tub-like pram around the neighbourhood and beyond, in search of rags. The female citizen continued to mingle curses with the dank odours of the airwell and to break startlingly out of the hotel at dawn into the quiet street. The rest of the tenants prostrated themselves before their old habits – or, if they were new tenants, brought new or old habits to the hotel. And then, quite abruptly, it was the early spring of a certain year.

The end came quickly. One day all was as usual. And on the next day it happened.

Lili, in the midst of her chore, had the sudden ungovernable impression that the holy man was dead. The atmosphere in his little black box contained a new and frightening element. She sniffed, and her skin prickled. Taking the chamber pot to a light part of the staircase, she found that it was empty. She returned at once to the room and spoke quietly and urgently at what she believed to be the holy man. It had apparently stopped breathing. There was, as usual, no response. But this time, with an irrepressible sense that something had changed, she put her hand forwards and touched. She drew it back quickly. What she had touched she did not understand. With trembling hands she lit a match. At this point she uttered one long, blood-curdling scream and hurtled downstairs as fast as her short fat legs would carry her. She reached the room which used to be the bar before anyone had time to intercept her. Locked fast there, and in spite of the loud knocking that came sporadically to her from the outside, she was able to slip out of the hotel at dusk, having spoken to no one of her experience.

Liza ran off that same night with a sailor from Marseille, and Greta, the biggest but most buxomly beautiful of the three, moved up to Pigalle, where (in nights that followed), under myriad coruscations of colour, her flesh gleamed whitely and naked in a darkened nightclub. She left barely an hour after Liza.

Mme Kronis had taken control of the tenants. There was an uncanny power in the woman. None of the other tenants was allowed to see the attic where, according to Mme Kronis, the holy man, poor soul, lay dead.

The following day there was the funeral. Mme Kronis, the thin Hungarian, one blind man and the woman with one foot missing turned out to follow the coffin.

Mme Kronis, now that the German women were gone, decided to reopen the bar. Meanwhile, she let it be known that there was one key available.

Peter Pierce

MY ONLY CONTACT with the outside world during my period of "retirement" was through the ragman. He lived in a room above mine at the back of the house. He was called Peter Pierce.

He was a small man with an obvious limp. His brown-bristled chin was as sharp as a knife, and it was always tilted to enable him to see better with his one eye. His other eye had been removed by a surgeon, skilfully, in an operating theatre which he described to me. The blind side of his face had a vacant, stricken look, almost supplicating, like the profile of a saint in an early Renaissance painting. Where the eye should have been was a concave tub of flesh, an empty socket, shiny and violet-pink, which looked as though it had been made by somebody pressing his thumb downward and inward from the bridge of the nose where the skin had a hurt, stretched appearance. He was really very ugly.

I told him I had to stay out of the way for a while because some men were looking for me. I had put something over on them and I had to lie low for a while. I told him I would pay him something if he would buy my food for me each day. He said there was no need for that. He would do it anyway out of friendship. But as he always insisted that I eat the evening meal with him, I said I would pay for it for the two of us, and he agreed to that. We ate upstairs in his room, and sometimes he brought a bottle of beer.

His room was crammed with an assortment of junk. A bundle of assorted rugs, old newspapers tied neatly into bales, pots, vases, busts, broken clocks and stacks of books. I was glad of the books.

I borrowed a few each day to read while he was out on his rounds.

He told me that he liked reading himself, but that he couldn't read much, because with only one eye he found it a bit of a strain. He was sorry about this, because one of the busts he had was a bust of Carlyle, and he had noticed that there were some of his books in the pile. He asked me if I didn't think that having a life-size bust in front of you of the man whose books you were reading wouldn't give you a clearer impression of what the man was like who wrote the books. I said I had never thought about it, but that I supposed there was something in what he said, for the books a man writes are part of his behaviour. He nodded his head eagerly. He said he wouldn't mind, some time, if it wouldn't bore me, hearing what Carlyle had written, because ever since he had had the bust he had wondered. If I would read to him, he would be very grateful.

But we agreed to leave it off for a while, for at least a week, because that week his round was on the other side of the town, and by the time he got back and cooked supper for us there was only enough time left to check up on what he'd collected and sort the rags and papers into bundles. I suggested that I could do the baling during the day, while he was out collecting. He was delighted about this.

That night, before I went downstairs to my own room, he had cooked some kippers for us, and afterwards, while we sat back and drank the beer which he'd bought, he suggested that he would be willing to have me as a partner in the business. I could do the sorting and baling like I said, and he would do the collecting and the selling. The proper disposal of the goods was important, he said, but for the moment at least he himself would attend to that. I wouldn't need to go out of the house at all.

There was only one thing. He could use a bit more capital, because sometimes he couldn't afford to buy what he was offered.

I said it seemed only fair to me that I should put some capital into the business, because, after all, he was doing the hard work and there was already a lot of stock in the room.

"In the future we can use your room too," he said.

That had not occurred to me, but I agreed, because, although some of the stuff that he brought in smelt rather strongly, I didn't see how I could reasonably object to the arrangement.

I asked him then how much he thought would be fair for me to pay into the business.

He considered that for a few moments, and then he asked me if I thought six pounds would be too much.

I told him that I thought it was quite reasonable, and so I gave him the money, and he insisted on giving me a receipt, on which he stated that I was now a full partner in the business. He always liked to have things in writing, he said, if it were in any way connected with business. You knew where you stood, then. And he asked me whether I was satisfied with the receipt. He was looking at me questioningly.

I told him I was, and I suggested that, as I would be doing the baling, we ought to store the paper in my room and the miscellaneous stuff in his. I think he was glad I suggested that, because while I was speaking I noticed he was eyeing the busts as though he feared I were going to suggest that he should part with them. But when I was returning to my own room, he insisted that I should take one of the busts with me, because he had noticed my room was pretty bare. "A man likes an ornament," he said.

I thanked him and said that I would begin the baling next day.

In the morning, one of the first things which gradually took shape in the growing light was the bust of the nameless man, one of whose ears was broken off and whose vacant eyes were towards me as I fell into sleep.

In the days that followed, I spent part of my time baling paper.

It was not long before I realized that it was not a flourishing business, that the stock upstairs in Peter's room was the accumulation of many months' work and that day by day he added very little to what was already there. At first I suspected he was no longer bringing back all he collected and that he was disposing of the greater part of it without my knowledge, and before he returned home in the evening. As he had told me he kept accounts, I asked to see those for the past six months, thinking that the sudden decline in the business would show and that when I pointed it out to him he would realize that I wasn't a person to be trifled with. I expected him to be reluctant to show me his books – and if he were, or if he refused outright to do so, I would know immediately that my suspicions were correct.

But it didn't happen like that. He was actually pleased when I asked him. He confided in me that he had been wondering, over the past few days, if he had made a mistake in accepting as a partner a man who was so foolish as to put up capital without wanting to see the books of the business in which he was investing. That had not seemed very business-like to him.

I was taken back by his directness and admitted that I had been guilty of an oversight when I made my original investment. I hastened to add that I was not usually like that, and was so on that occasion only because he was my friend and because I had trusted him implicitly.

He looked at the floor while I said this, and when he saw that I hadn't anything further to say, he said that it was very kind of me to trust him in that way on such a short acquaintance, that that thought – and he felt ashamed of himself – had not occurred to him, which only went to show that his first impression of me had been correct: that I was a man of feeling.

I thanked him for saying so.

He said that on the contrary I had every right to be angry with him. He felt thoroughly ashamed of himself. It was unpardonable of him to have judged me at all, and it was criminal of him to have overlooked the most important factor in the situation. He hoped I would forgive him, that he hadn't lost my friendship because of it.

I assured him there was no danger of that, that to turn away from him on such a flimsy pretext would be to commit a much greater impetuosity of judgement that he had been guilty of.

He looked at me for a few moments without speaking, and then he said that I was very young to speak so wisely, that it had taken him much longer to learn that lesson and that even now, as I had seen, he was sometimes guilty of falling into his old ways.

We didn't speak for some time after that. Neither of us felt there was anything to be added. And then, suddenly, he remembered that I had asked to see the books of the business. He hoped that I would not find them too untidy, and that, if there were any mistakes, I would not be too embarrassed to point them out. He found close work very difficult with only one eye – and that not as good as it used to be. He limped over to the wardrobe and brought three massive ledgers out from the interior. They were half bound in faded red leather with the numbers 1, 2 and 3 inscribed in gold on their spines. It was only then that it occurred to me that he must have been a very old man.

"I don't suppose you'll want much more than a glance at the first two," he said. "There's not much of interest for you there. Two of the busts, I think, and some odd bits and pieces and a few of the books that didn't get sold the last time I had a clearance."

I asked him what period the three ledgers covered.

He didn't remember exactly, he said, but we could soon look and see, because he had always taken great care to enter the correct dates.

We opened the first ledger. The pages were yellow with age, and the ink had faded to an anonymous, neutral sepia colour. The date at the top of the first page was "15th August 1901".

"Ascension Day," he said. "I should have remembered. I bought very little, as you can see for yourself."

Under the date was the following inventory:

One clock (broken) . . . . *3d.*

Rags (various) . . . . *1d.*

One etching of a castle (unknown) signed

"E. Prout" and dated 1872 (interesting) . . . . *¾d.*

Total 4 ¾d.

"That etching," he said. "I almost decided to specialize in artworks, etchings and busts, you know. You'll notice I didn't buy anything for two days after that. I had to think." He drew a half-smoked cigarette from his vest pocket and lit it. "I decided against it," he went on after he had lit it. "Yes, I decided against it." He turned over the pages of the first ledger away from his decision, and then he said I could look through the first two at my leisure the following day, that it was the third one which concerned us. The first entry was dated "28th October 1940".

"Hallowe'en," he said. "The war was on."

It didn't take me long to notice that on many days he didn't appear to have bought anything at all. I questioned him about it. He mumbled something about having enough, about not wanting to overstock himself. I turned quickly to recent business. The articles bought consisted mostly of old paper and rags, but even those he appeared to buy in ludicrously small quantities. It occurred to me that it was strange, considering the present limited business, that he should have decided to take on a partner, especially one like myself who was willing only to bale and pack what he collected, and I could think of no earthly reason why he should want more capital for a business which had not only begun to dry up over the last few years, but which he didn't appear to have any intention of expanding.

He was watching me apprehensively, his head tilted like a bird's, his elbows stuck to his thin knees as he leant forwards in his chair and followed my progress from page to page; occasionally he made a vague reference to how he had disposed of this item or that, pointing to where it was recorded with the forefinger of his right hand. He apologized more than once for his handwriting, which was most exact and copperplate. He appeared, in spite of his modesty, to be the perfect clerk. What struck me as absurd was the inordinate care which he lavished on the most trivial transactions.

I asked him as casually as I could in what direction he intended to expand the business with the capital which I had invested. He considered the question for a moment before answering, and then he said that of course there were a number of possibilities, but that the main thing for any business, especially of this nature, was to possess an adequate reserve of floating capital. You never knew, he said, when you would require it.

I admitted that that seemed reasonable enough, but pointed out that if we could judge from the records over the last few years, we were hardly likely to be called upon to produce so much money at one time.

He said that that was as it might be, but that it didn't prove anything. The very next day he might go out and find that he needed not six pounds, but seven. He was obstinate in his refusal to draw any conclusions from the fact that during the past few years he had never bought more than three shillings' worth of goods in one day, and he gradually became more irritable when he realized that I wasn't satisfied with his explanations. I could feel his resentment as I turned back idly over the pages of the third volume, and, not wanting to quarrel with him, I suggested that there would be plenty of time in the future for us to discuss the business, and that for the moment I was quite satisfied and felt like going to bed. His irritation left him immediately I said this, and he suggested that I should have a cup of cocoa before I went downstairs.

He boiled water on a little alcohol burner whose flame was blue and almost transparent, as though there were no density of heat there to raise the temperature of the uncovered water. The little pot was perched precariously on three flame-blackened tin spokes, and it steamed gently, for a long time, below boiling point. The light in the room was a poor one. The wallpaper, dark during the day – heavy fawn anastomosed by tendrils of flowers, berries, leaves, all brown – was darker now, dark at the corners to the point of extinction; and as Peter stood watching the flame and the pot of water as though he knew what to expect, yet inquisitive – bending low to consider the flame and then peering into the pot, and nervous at the same time – I had the feeling of not belonging there... of being a disruptive influence in a place whose century and whole orientation were not mine, stared at by the ridiculous busts with no eyes, and with three massive and indecipherable ledgers on the table in front of me, which were indecipherable not because I could not add or subtract or follow the entries, but because, having done so, I was unable to grasp their significance: I could see right through them and, having done so, had an irresistible feeling that I had somehow missed the point. Peter still tended the flame and seemed preoccupied. He did not speak. If it had not been for a nervousness which seemed to attach to his gesture of waiting, I would have thought that he had forgotten I was in the room with him. But as it was, it was obvious that he hadn't. It occurred to me that for some reason or other he did not trust himself to speak. His lips were set over the pale pink gums, in which a row of brown stake-like teeth were embedded, unevenly, and in the lower jaw only. He was making cocoa.

He wanted to be involved in that to be free of me. Simultaneously, he wanted to be doing something for me. I supposed it was his way of showing his disapproval and of signifying at the same time that in spite of it he still considered himself my friend, my partner. I wondered if he realized how unfamiliar everything was to me. I was aware of nothing familiar in the room. Everything – Peter himself, the miscellaneous objects – was trivial, gratuitously so, and yet, somehow, because he was so clearly involved, portentous. It was like a puppet show, but, disturbingly, the puppets moved by themselves. I could see only from the outside. I watched him grow impatient. And then, after a moment's hesitation, he stirred the brown powder into the water. While he was doing it, the realization came to me that that was not the best way to make cocoa – that cocoa tended to form into lumps if sprinkled into hot water – and I wanted to tell him about it, and then found that I could not, because unaccountably it came over me that I must be wrong. And yet, all the time that I didn't speak, I knew that I was not.

"Here it is," he said at last, removing it from the flame. He went on stirring it as he carried it steaming and still unboiled to the table. "You can put the books on the floor," he said. "I'll put them away afterwards."

I put the ledgers, one on top of the other, at my feet, and he placed two cups in front of us and filled them with the cocoa, which was thin and watery like tea, on the surface of which the pinheads of undissolved powder (which I had predicted when I watched his ineffectual efforts to stir it in) floated like minute balls of dark wet sand. He spilt a little on the table, and wiped it away with a crumpled red handkerchief, which he found in the side pocket of his jacket.

"Bad pourer," he said apologetically.

I nodded.

"It's not sweetened," he said then. "I haven't got any sugar."

I said that it didn't matter, that that was the way I liked it, and we sat opposite one another waiting for it to cool a little, before we drank. He said that he liked cocoa, because it made him sleep well, that sometimes in the middle of the night, because of his insomnia – his mother too had been troubled by insomnia – he would work a bit on the ledgers.

"There's always something to do," you know, he said.

He liked to make all the entries with a soft pencil first, a 3B, because it rubbed out easily, and then only afterwards, when he had rechecked his figures and studied the inventory, to go over it in ink. For this latter operation he liked to use a penholder and a steel nib selected from an old lozenge box in which he kept many nibs of various thicknesses, shapes and pliabilities, each of which, after it had been used, was wiped carefully on a pen-wiper which he had made himself out of four absorbent pieces of rag, circular in shape and sewn together at the centre with a trouser button at either side. He wanted to show me his nibs, he said, and he got up with his cocoa untouched and went over to the wardrobe. He returned with a cardboard shoebox, which he placed on the table in front of him as he sat down again. From the shoe box he took the lozenge box, and from the interior of that, which had been lined with tissue paper, he poured a small heap of pen nibs onto the table. As they tinkled onto the wood, his eyes lit up. The nibs were gold and silver and blue and brown. He selected one of the gold ones, which had two tubes on its underside, and passed it over to me, smiling.

"It's a newfangled one," he said. His tone was deprecatory. "It's supposed to hold enough ink for five hundred words. It always blots."

He said that it was a good thing that he made a practice of testing all new nibs before he risked using them on the ledgers, and I agreed with him.

"It always blots," he said again. "I don't know why I keep it. I've been meaning to throw it away ever since I got it."

But he took it back from me nevertheless, and dropped it back into the lozenge box. He went on to explain the merits of each nib, holding them up in turn for me to look at them, but without allowing me to touch them. This reluctance to let me look at them for myself annoyed me slightly. I don't know why, unless it was because it seemed to prohibit my becoming as interested as he was. Whenever I made a gesture to accept whatever nib he was holding up to the light for me to examine, the spear- or spade-shaped point, the contour of the slit or hole, he moved it hastily back towards the lozenge box and dropped it in. I became more and more exasperated, and finally, having had enough of it, I said rather rudely that his cocoa was getting cold.

He pricked back his ears momentarily, as though he hadn't caught what I said, and then all of a sudden he smiled and thanked me for reminding him. He didn't like it too hot, but he didn't like it too cold either, he said. And then, after taking two or three tentative sips and showing his toothless upper gum, he confided that he always selected the nib he was going to use on a particular occasion with great care. It was more exact that way, he said. Although I couldn't quite follow what he meant, I said that I supposed it was, and he said again, "Oh yes, it's more exact."

After that, we drank for a while without speaking.

He closed the lozenge box and returned it to the shoebox, whose other contents he had taken great care to hide from me, and then, as though he had forgotten that he had asked me before, he asked me what I thought about the ledgers. He hoped I was satisfied with them, he said, and when I said I was, he nodded his head and said that he had known all along that I would be, but that it was a relief to have my personal assurance on the point. Apart altogether from the fact that I was his partner and that naturally he wanted me to be satisfied, he was glad to have had an opportunity to hear a second opinion. He had always considered that important, although up till then he had not had sufficient confidence in anyone to show the ledgers. One had to be careful.

I agreed. I asked him what reason he had for trusting me. It was hard to say, he said. But he had felt quite sure from the beginning.

I thanked him without enthusiasm. I was tired. I had finished my cocoa, which I hadn't enjoyed. As I stood up to go, I wondered what his attitude towards me would be if he knew that I was wanted by the police. I was no longer surprised by his lack of comment on the fact some men were supposed to be looking for me. He accepted it, believed it, and there the matter ended for him. He was not interested.

Nothing could have suited me better.

When we said goodnight, he shook my hand warmly and said that he would be going out as usual the next day. And then, looking round and scratching his head, he said something about having a clearance soon.

I said that I trusted his judgement, that he had had more experience, after all, and that seemed to please him. He leant over the banister solicitously as I went downstairs to my room.

I was bored and restless. I read a book for a while, and afterwards fried an egg. I wasn't hungry. But to prepare it and then to eat it gave me something to do. When I had finished, I spent five minutes cleaning the frying pan with old newspapers. They were more than ten years old, yellow, and the urgency of the print seemed futile, like poses in an old snapshot.

I had been over three weeks in the house, and I had already decided that it would be safe to leave the town by train the next day. I had said nothing of my intentions to Peter. Somehow, I felt, he wouldn't be convinced. During three weeks I had come to realize that the world of police and petty criminals like myself – indeed the entire world – did not exist for him, or only in a strange, oblique way. It was not that he would have worried about my safety. He was hardly conscious of my danger. I felt merely that my decision to leave him and our partnership would be beyond his comprehension. At the same time, I was inquisitive to know what he did during the long hours he was supposed to be out collecting rags and papers. It was that which decided me to follow him.

It was after ten o'clock on the following morning when I heard him come downstairs past my landing and go out. My own bag was already packed, and I had left a short letter for him thanking him for his kindness and apologizing for my sudden departure. I was able to watch him from the window. He hesitated on the street outside, and then, as though something had just occurred to him, he made off to the left up the street. He was carrying a small brown paper bag, and he was not walking quickly.

A few moments later I was following him at a distance of about twenty yards. The first thing that struck me was that he didn't appear to be going anywhere in particular. He frequently turned off at right angles, almost re-crossing his path, and he hesitated for a long time at each major crossing. From behind, his thick grey trousers had a corrugated appearance. They were too long in the legs for him. His feet made a shuffling sound as they walked, clad in warped brown shoes whose uppers were broken and split. He wore a navy-blue serge jacket, which was gone at the cuffs and elbows, and a ridiculously wide-brimmed grey fedora hat. I wondered what was in the paper bag. I trailed him closely. In that way, I felt, the people would notice him rather than me – the hat, the paper bag, the shambling, corrugated walk.

It was a fine morning, and the streets were quite crowded. Sometimes, momentarily, I lost sight of him, and once I nearly lost him altogether when he turned a corner suddenly without my noticing him. I hesitated at the crossroads, and was about to go off in the wrong direction when I saw him coming back along the pavement towards me. I stepped back out of sight into a shop doorway, and a moment later he was hesitating at the corner a few yards away. Finally, he crossed the street and followed the main thoroughfare towards the park.

As I followed him into the park, I wondered what possible motive he could have for going there. The park was almost empty. Most men of my age were at work, and those who weren't were conspicuous. I was rather annoyed with myself for following him there. Two young men and a girl passed me on the footpath – students, I supposed, because they were carrying books. When they saw me, they stopped laughing, and for a moment I thought they had recognized me. But then they were past me and laughing again, the voice of one of the men coming back to me – high, artificial and excited – as though he were mimicking someone, and then the girl's laughter again. I turned to watch her. She was walking between them, swinging a pot-shaped handbag on a long leather strap, in flat shoes and summer dress, and strikingly blonde, her hair rising gracefully from her neck in a ribboned horsetail. She was slim-hipped and desired obviously by both of them.

It struck me suddenly how foolish I had been to be alarmed. Apart from some policemen, there was no possibility of anyone's recognizing me.

Peter was climbing a patch which led uphill, more like a windmill than a man. There was something unsettling about him. I was not able to put my finger on it until later. What was familiar was the familiarity of limbs out of control, of something missing which should have been there – the absence of which, more telling than what remains, strikes at one deeply, almost person-ally, making one feel that one is face to face with the subhuman. The dead are like that, and the maimed – and Peter was. As he moved upwards towards the skyline, a triangle of white morning light dangled between the raking black legs, and the hoop of his back and his arms twisted hori-zontally like a tuberous root above them, and the head, a nob under the broad hat rim, looked in no direction, as though direction were irrelevant now, and the park and the traffic beyond on the road and the people who walked there were irrelevant too, all except the gratuitous movement in which he was involved and which was not his own, because the man was absent from it.

When I came to the crest of the hill, I looked down on the duck pond. He was there, leaning forwards across the railing, in one of this hands the brown paper bag from which he extracted bread, which he fed gently to four squawking ducks. He was too engrossed in what he was doing to notice me. I watched for a few minutes without moving, and then, as I did not wish him to recognize me, I turned and walked slowly away. It was nearly noon. The train left from the Central Station in fifty minutes. I would be able to catch it. My last sight of Peter sticks in my memory. He had removed his wide-brimmed hat and was mopping with his red handkerchief his forehead beneath his thin, wind-blown hair.

A Meeting

REMEMBERING ALL MANNER of things, faces, voices, smells, situations, which he knew but which he had forgotten – almost, he thought, as though he had tricked himself into forgetting them, marks of fear or shame erased from his memory as from a diary, a bed or a room, because he no longer wanted them, because they were irrelevant, because they threatened his present identity – he was aware of his own rejection of them, but he was aware of it only indirectly in the vague irritation which he felt at the sight of his colleagues, who had scarcely existed for him the day before, or at the sight of the blot which clung to the tail of the last figure in the column of figures in front of him.

He would have liked to take off his jacket and the tie, which was knotted in a tiny red knot, close, at his throat, but he put the thought away from him again, because it was impossible with old Beakin sitting there and one of the partners, Mr Alan Curtis or young Mr Fenton, likely to come in at any moment.

Since ten o'clock in the morning, the heat had been unbearable. His lunch in the smoke room of the restaurant across the street had been hot, colourless, tasteless. Stewed rabbit at one and ninepence, all bones. Susie, the waitress, agreed with him, strongly enough to suggest that she considered the affront a personal one. *And us girls* (the waitresses) *doin'* our best to keep you regular gentlemen satisfied. It was the new cook, she said. She couldn't boil water without singeing it. He could still see the fork lying in cold gravy, little beads of solidified fat on the prongs. Susie removed the plate with her red hand. Afterwards, he had walked about the streets for a while, but it was so hot, and the streets were so crowded with people going and coming from lunch, that he had returned to the office early.

He found himself resenting the sun. It sprawled across the papers in front of him and glinted painfully in the lenses of his spectacles. It was a nuisance. He felt a similar vague resentment against the fat, round buttocks of Miss Eileen Lanelly tightening under a shiny blue serge skirt as she bent down to pick up a pencil from the floor. She had a habit of dropping things. And today she had made a mistake in one of the ledgers.

"Really, Miss Lanelly," Beakin had said. "In the six years you've been with us I have learnt to expect more accuracy from you. Such a trifling mistake! What would the auditors say?"

Miss Lanelly had supported from childhood an air of conscious guilt. Mr Beakin was inspired by it and fed on it like a bird.

"I can't help it, Mr Beakin, it's so terribly hot! I can't concentrate in all this heat."

"The work must go on, Miss Lanelly," Mr Beakin said in his thin, sour-sweet way. "Perhaps if you were to open the window…"

The window was open now, and a wall of stale city-spent air moved in with the sunlight. The broad world of Miss Lanelly diminished as she straightened up and moved over to the filing cabinet.

A fly settled on the back of his hand. He became interested in its movement, in the dull veined lustre of its minute wings and its black button-like eyes – flat, built outwards like two headlamps; he wondered what it would look like through a microscope, and then he became aware that Mr Beakin was watching him, and he allowed his eyes to be drawn back towards the papers on his desk. The suggestion of a sex life for Miss Lanelly intrigued him. It was, he was sure, a small sex life, an insectal one, almost non-existent, irritant rather than active, and smothered in tweeds – blind, impotent, diminutive, sunk, like a crippled ant beneath a clod of earth, in the amorphous mass of flesh which she appeared to have bundled each morning with some difficulty into her clothes.

A moment ago, surreptitiously, she had slipped something into her mouth. A piece of chocolate, he supposed. He had seen the silver paper and the crushed wrapper in her wastepaper basket. She was fond of chocolate.

The sun fell on Mr Beakin and on the fly and on the inkpots and pens and on the two other male clerks, Riley and Wilson. It inclined in a wedge towards the filing cabinet, where Miss Lanelly pretended to be looking for something.

He brushed the fly away and looked at his thumbnail. The noise of the traffic came up from the street through the open window. A wasp landed suddenly on the ledger, crawled a few inches and then flew out again into the sunlight.

Mr Beakin coughed, and Riley whispered something to Wilson. He couldn't hear what they were saying. He looked without interest at them. James Fidler didn't like his colleagues, and seldom spoke to them. He nodded to them each morning as he came in, and then he ignored them as completely as possible. The two clerks were a tiresome pair, always amused in a silly, secretive way. It had always struck him as ludicrous that five people with so little in common could pass the greater part of their waking lives together filing, indexing, keeping the ledgers in order. He supposed they all had their reasons. For Beakin, who was over sixty, it had been a career. For Fidler himself it was "part of the routine"; he had always considered it, or avoided considering it, in those vague terms. Riley and Wilson were grown-up schoolboys. They went to football matches on Saturday afternoons. The office was a job for them. They were free at five thirty. And Miss Lanelly, professedly, "needed the money". As though they all didn't. But Miss Lanelly appeared to be convinced that she needed the money in a different way: the rest of the staff worked, and it was proper that they should do so, but Miss Lanelly worked because she needed the money. God's oversight, perhaps. That impression he had gathered from conversations overheard.

The afternoon was nearly over. At five thirty he would catch a bus for the suburb in which he lived and he would eat his evening meal with his mother and his sister. It was an absurdity which he accepted, another one. Each evening he stepped onto a bus which took him to where he had never decided to be.

His sister appalled him – a frail, brittle orange woman in her late forties who had grown out of the gangly young woman whom he had surprised in the act of admiring herself in the long wardrobe mirror, and who, still naked and terrible, had come upon him in his room that night and wrestled with him on his bed. Neither his sister nor he had ever referred to the incident. They had always disliked each other. Looking at her now, it was difficult to believe it had ever happened.

Kate Fidler worked in a confectioner's shop; perhaps he disliked her more because of that. She was resigned. She respected "her betters", she was an obsequious woman who served candy and chocolate and toffees, and powdered her face with a very bright pink powder which caked into ugly little islands round her nose. She wore it because it was powder: "all ladies powdered themselves". She never used a mirror.

There was no conversation at table. Kate disapproved of him. He had no ambition, she said – but always to the other woman, the mother: she never spoke to him directly. And his mother's conversation was limited to her chronic arthritis. It was not a pleasant meal. That was why he had been so disappointed with the rabbit at lunchtime: he looked forward to his lunch in the smoke room. The evening meal was always the same. The grandmother clock ticked. Fidler looked at his plate, contemplating what was on it, tough little morsels of stewed meat or boiled cod, unappetizingly transparent like candles, conscious all the time of Kate's sniffing and of the low, sucking noise which came from his mother as she picked at her food. The house itself was shabby, anonymous, and an old female smell pervaded it.

The fly had disappeared. Out of the corner of his eye he watched Miss Lanelly move away from the filing cabinet.

"Have you finished it, James?" Beakin was saying.

"In a moment, Mr Beakin."

"I don't know what's come over the people in this office," the manager said generally, and glanced at the clock. "A little sun, and the whole routine goes to pot."

Miss Lanelly was grinning at him a knowing look now Beakin had turned his back. He felt uncomfortable and ignored her. As the "assistant manager" (it was not his official title, but he was the senior when Beakin was on holiday – "Ah, Fidler, of course!" Mr Alan Curtis would say on those occasions), he considered it impertinent of her. He laughed at his own feelings, but it was a question of habit. Miss Lanelly was a comparative newcomer, while Fidler himself had been with the firm for nearly twenty years; the miles of copperplate handwriting, the office stamps, the endless paper clips, were as much part of his past as the little scar above his right eye or as the few furtive adventures he had had with women. Eileen Lanelly's grin recalled those adventures to him: it was friendly; she was inviting him to share something with her, and he found himself resenting her offer.

He tried to concentrate on the figures in front of him, but they had become insignificant. His eye returned to the blot and stopped there. The fly was walking across the paper towards his hand. For a moment it held his attention, and then he began to think of his two weeks' holiday, which began the following Monday.

The sky was clouding over.

Mr Beakin put on his hat, and Riley and Wilson pretended to tidy up their desks. They were a smug pair.

"James," Mr Beakin said, "I wonder if you'd mind finishing that before you leave? If you're not in a hurry."

He nodded. He felt no inclination to get home quickly. "And you, Miss Lanelly, if you would put right that little mistake of yours in the ledger."

"Yes, Mr Beakin."

"Use the new eraser, Miss Lanelly. It doesn't make such an ugly mark as the old one."

"Yes, Mr Beakin." A singsong voice. Ten years too young for her.

Beakin ignored it. "Goodnight Riley, goodnight Wilson," he said. He caught Fidler's eye for a moment, and then he went out, humming.

When he had gone, Wilson winked at Riley.

"Don't forget to lock up, James!" Wilson said crookedly from under his little black moustache.

Riley grinned and slammed the lid of his desk. "Looks like rain," he said. "Thunder."

Fidler ignored them.

"Come, Riley," Wilson said, and they went out together. He listened to the neat, nasty voices as they died away in the corridor.

Wilson was married. Four years ago Fidler had donated five shillings towards his wedding present. He couldn't remember what it was they gave him – a metal object with a fatuous inscription.

Miss Lanelly turned towards him. They were alone now. "They think they're funny," she said, but he didn't answer. He appeared to be engrossed in the papers in front of him.

She walked over to the window and looked out.

When he looked up, she was lighting a cigarette. He noticed that one of her stockings was laddered just below and behind her knee; it disappeared under her skirt.

He felt a sudden desire to laugh.

"Don't be long with that ledger, Miss Lanelly," he said after a few moments. "I want to lock up."

She was still standing at the window, looking out, with the extinguished match in her hand. Riley and Wilson called her Eileen.

"Oh, damn Beakin!" she said. "I'll do it in the morning before he comes in. There's the rain on now, Mr Fidler. It's heavy."

The rain spattered in little bouncing drops on the window sill. Automatically he glanced over at the coat rack. He had not brought his umbrella, and he felt vaguely annoyed with himself; he seldom came out without an umbrella.

"Oh, God!" Miss Lanelly said. "What a day! First the sun and now this! I don't know why people stay in this filthy country! Were you ever in the south of France, Mr Fidler?"

"No." He put the cap on his fountain pen and replaced it in his pocket beside his pocket handkerchief.

"I was," she said. "I was in Nice and Monte Carlo. I can't understand why people stay here."

She was a heavy woman, as tall as he was, her clothes always giving the impression that she was held together by pins.

"Why do people stay anywhere or do anything?" he said. "Why do they?"

"Four pounds a week," she said. "That's easy!"

He gathered the papers together. "You could earn more elsewhere," he said.

"Oh, I don't know, there'd always be something. Rain in June. Just look at it!"

"There always is," he agreed. He looked at his watch.

"Just look at it!" she said again.

"It *is* heavy," he said, "but it won't last long."

Heavy rain never lasted for long; fine rain lasted for days. He had known that since he was a boy, like snowdrops in January and crocuses in February. He wondered how many times in his life he had said those exact words: "It *is* heavy, but it won't last…" as though he were enunciating a self-evident proposition.

"No, thank goodness," Miss Lanelly said.

Evidently it was part of her past too, part of her girlhood. It occurred to him that he did not know very much about Miss Lanelly. This is Miss Lanelly: she sings in our church choir. Miss Lanelly wears tight skirts and catches cold each March. She "needs the money". When she first came to the office, Riley had gone out with her once or twice – "for a lark" – but it had not come to anything, and now they were hardly on speaking terms. She was cold, Riley said.

"Beakin says I can't take my holidays till September this year," Miss Lanelly said. "Can you imagine that? Sit in this lousy place all through the summer and then two weeks, *two weeks* at the tail end!" She had taken out one of her hair clips and was holding it in her mouth while she combed her hair. "I felt like going to see old Curtis about it."

It was mouse-coloured hair.

"You'd have a better chance with Fenton."

She replaced the hair clip and laughed. "Oh, no, not him! You know what he said? 'If you'll just speak to Mr Beakin about it, Miss Lanelly, I'm sure he will accommodate you.' Can you imagine that? Fenton! He's scared to death of Beakin!"

Fidler smiled. It was the first time in six years that he had really talked to Miss Lanelly. He liked her explosiveness – it was fresh, feminine. And she wasn't old. He found himself wandering what it would be like to make love to her.

"Are you ready?" he said. "I want to lock up now."

"Lock up? Why? What is there to steal? A few mouldy accounts!"

"And the new eraser," he said.

She laughed. "Oh, I'm ready when you are, I'll do the ledger in the morning."

"Good."

It gave him pleasure, somehow, to be in on this defiance of Mr Beakin. It had never occurred to him to be defiant himself, any more than it had ever occurred to him to lodge apart from his mother and his sister. It was not that he had Kate's resignation, which was indulgent: he accepted Mr Beakin and the order he represented from habit, without committing himself, because his desire to rebel was no stronger than his desire to submit; he could find no motive in himself to do either. Kate's abject triumph, the certainty that spoke through thin, old-woman's lips, sickened him. It was unhealthy. Miss Lanelly's bubbling impertinence was refreshing.

She put away her powder compact, arranged the white bow at her neck, and they walked down the stairs together to the street door. The rain was still coming down heavily, ringing whitely on the pavements. It occurred to him that it had been raining for precisely ten minutes.

"It can't last," she said, glancing up the street.

Except for the traffic, it was almost deserted. A few people with umbrellas were still walking about, leaning forwards against the rain. Others crowded in shop doorways. He heard his lips saying "tut tut" in vexation.

Miss Lanelly giggled. "It's like a shower bath," she said.

"A monsoon."

"What did you say?"

"A monsoon," he said.

"Oh, I thought you said it would stop soon…"

"I like the rain," he said.

She didn't answer him. Perhaps she hadn't heard him. The rain continued to fall in front of them like a sparkling bead curtain. Little gushers of water rose from under the wheels of passing tramcars.

It occurred to him to invite her for a drink.

"We might as well," Miss Lanelly said. "It'd be better than standing here, anyway. It's got cold suddenly."

"It'll be warm again after the rain," he said. "It won't do any harm."

"Oh, I like the rain," she said, "but let's go now. There's a bar opposite, isn't there?"

"Yes, the Royal."

"We'll make a dash for it," she said. "Here, come under this." She held her thin plastic waterproof over their heads. "You hold the other end of it."

He did so, and when he had turned up his collar with his free hand, they ran across the street together and through the revolving doorway.

"Oh my God!" she said, breathless and laughing. "I'm soaked!" She looked down at herself. "Damn! I've laddered my stocking!"

Miss Lanelly, sipping her sherry, felt comfortable for the first time that day.

The bar was crowded, hot and damp from the damp garments of the customers. It was nearly six o'clock. Fidler was drinking whisky and listening absently for the rain to stop. He was conscious of himself in the wall mirror, a thin man in spectacles, unprepossessing, with a permanent stoop and still wearing his discoloured soft hat; and the profile of the woman beside him – he could feel the heat of her body close to his own – soft-jowled, the lips big, and the soft grey eyes embedded like humorous buttons in her fleshy face, excited him. She smelt of wet clothes and make-up and woman.

"Do you live far?" Miss Lanelly asked.

"Not far – about twenty minutes in the bus, a few stops after East Park."

"Oh."

She was looking at him almost conspiratorially, and he felt attracted and repelled at the same time: big and soft and clumsy. "Our elephant," Riley called her once with that prurient little snigger of his. Riley had the face of a fox, red and pointed.

Fidler was thoughtful. The "oh" had been non-committal. He wondered whether she had asked merely out of politeness.

"And you?"

"There's the thunder again," she said.

It was a loud clap: it broke slowly into the crowded bar. For a moment everyone was silent, and then the glasses clinked and laughter broke out again.

"Ominous, isn't it?"

It was a stupid thing to say, he felt, because it wasn't at all ominous. That was not what he had meant to say. The word had sprung to his lips simply because he had wanted to be the first to break the silence; it was as though any word would have done.

"When I was a girl I used to be afraid of it," she said. "I thought it was a kind of earthquake. I knew a man once who was struck by lightning."

He supposed she was lying, making it up, but he didn't care, because most conversation appeared to him in that light – false, artificial, a game of adjustment within the world of another in which what was said was insignificant, the end being to intrude oneself, ineffaceably, to make the other recognize one's existence.

"Was he killed?"

"The man? Oh yes, he was killed all right, *instantaneously*. But I was only a girl at the time. I wasn't allowed to see him."

"Did you want to?" Fidler was wondering what a man struck by lightning would look like. Electrocuted. Like they did to murderers in America.

"I really don't know whether I did or not," Miss Lanelly said. "I don't remember. It's funny, but I don't remember. All I know is my father went to his funeral."

"Do you live with your parents now?"

"Oh, no. They're both dead. I've got a furnished room."

"You're lucky," he said. "I live with my mother and sister."

Kate would be home now, and they would be preparing the meal. They would be annoyed at his being late.

"Oh, I don't know," she said. "It gets a bit lonely at times with only Mrs Whelan to talk to. She's my landlady. She's Irish. And I don't get out much, because I don't know many people here. Except those at the choir. They're funny. You should see them."

"Then it's true – you do sing in a choir? I thought Riley was making it up."

She was no longer smiling.

"Yes," she said. "I sing in a choir. I like singing. I don't like Riley. I think he's a fool."

Fidler nodded. "What do you sing? I mean, what are you?"

"Alto," she said. "We sing hymns and anthems, mostly."

"In church?"

"Twice on Sundays. Practice once a week. Tonight, as a matter of fact. Tuesdays."

For some reason or other, Fidler felt uncomfortable. People who practised religion always made him feel that way. He considered them insane.

"What's wrong?" Miss Lanelly said.

"Oh, nothing," he said. "It seems funny, that's all. You believing in God and all that."

"Who said anything about God?" Miss Lanelly said. "I sing in church. I like singing, and they pay me a guinea a week for it."

"Then you don't believe in God?"

She laughed. "I think if He existed it would be necessary to murder Him! No, I don't believe. I believe in precious little. In myself, in people sometimes..."

"Yes," Fidler said. He was interrupted by the waitress, who arrived with new drinks. He paid for them and went on: "But it's difficult with other people. There's a kind of 'as if' quality about their actions. I mean, one acts oneself, but other people only act 'as if' – one never really knows."

She laughed. "I know what you mean," she said. "It's true. But it's the same for everyone."

"Only, some people don't recognize it," Fidler said. "They take it for granted that they can know other people."

"Yes," Miss Lanelly said. "You know I went out twice with Riley when I first came to the office. He said he didn't think there was any problem of communication in the twentieth century. He said we had cinema, radio and television. He couldn't understand why I wouldn't let him sleep with me."

She held her sherry up to the light, looked at it closely and then drank.

"I'll be drunk for choir practice!" she laughed.

She had put another cigarette in her mouth. He lit it for her. The noise of the rain had diminished; some of the people were moving towards the door.

"Why don't you move?" she said suddenly, blowing the first breath of smoke upwards from the fat part of her lower lip. "If you don't like staying with your family, you can surely move?"

"I'd have to want to first, I suppose. I don't know. I never really thought about it."

"You can't want to move very badly," Miss Lanelly said. "It's up to you, after all."

He had the impression that she was drifting away from him. The neon lighting in the bar was hurting his eyes. One of the long helio globes was flickering – something wrong with the connection.

"I don't want anything very badly," Fidler said. "It's rather pointless," and, saying it, he felt false.

"If that's true, it's you that's lucky," Miss Lanelly said. "My God, I want so many things badly!"

"Perhaps it's not true," he said quickly. He found himself alarmed at the thought of losing abruptly the vague sense of physical intimacy he derived from sitting close to her in the hot, crowded room. "I mean, it may be just that I don't know, and meanwhile it's as though I were living in abeyance."

"The rain's off," a voice said.

Two men squeezed past Fidler's chair. He moved forwards to facilitate their exit.

"I thought it would be different after the war," Miss Lanelly said suddenly. "But it's not, it's the same. Worse, if anything."

"How do you mean?"

"Oh, I don't know. It should have been different, somehow."

Fidler said nothing. It was as though whatever he said would be false.

She looked at her watch and said that Mrs Whelan would be wondering where she was.

"Yes, the rain seems to be off." He finished his whisky and stood up.

He asked her what church she sang in.

"Limepark Congregational," she said. "And for goodness' sake, stop calling me Miss Lanelly. You've known me for six years now!"

He smiled and took her arm to lead her through the crowd. He was about to tell her to call him James, then didn't. He was going to put the matchbox in his pocket, but it was empty, so he threw it away.

Notes

p. 14, *in vitam æternam*: "To eternal life" (Latin).

p. 15, *Perducat nos in vitam æternam*: "May He bring us to eternal life" (Latin).

CALDER PUBLICATIONS
EDGY TITLES FROM A LEGENDARY LIST